Justin,

Happy Valentines Day!

Mom & Dad
Ian

2-14-81

The Turtles' Picnic
and Other Nonsense Stories

adapted by Terry Berger • pictures by Erkki Alanen

Crown Publishers, Inc.
New York

Drawn for my favorite kids
Kirsti and Pentti   E.A.

The text of this book is set in 18 point Baskerville.
The illustrations are pen and ink drawings with wash overlays prepared by the artist and
printed in three colors.

Library of Congress Cataloging in Publication Data
Berger, Terry.
   The turtles' picnic and other nonsense stories.
   Summary: Three short stories about a suspicious
turtle, a very particular dog, and the king of the jungle.
   [1. Short stories. 2. Humorous stories] I. Alanen,
Erkki. II. Title.
PZ7.B45215Tu3   [E]   77-3309   ISBN 0-517-52998-X

contents

The Turtles' Picnic

Once upon a time there were three
turtles, Father, Mother, and Baby.
One fine day they decided to have a picnic.
First they agreed on a place to go,
a forest, far, far away.

Then they began to pack their baskets with
cans of tuna and cans of beans and cucumber
sandwiches and blueberry ices and everything
else they could think of.

Three months later they finished packing

and started on their way.

They walked and walked.

Three years later they reached the forest.

They began to unpack their baskets.

First they laid a cloth on the ground.

Then they laid out the food.

But just as they were about to eat,

Mother said, "Stop! We forgot to bring

the can opener."

She turned the baskets upside down
and shook them around and around.
Mother looked at Father. Father looked
at Mother. They both looked at Baby.
"Baby," they said, "you will have to go
back and get it."
"No," said Baby.

"We need it," said Mother.

"It can't be helped," said Father.

"Then," said Baby, "do you swear, do you promise, that you won't touch a thing until I get back?"

"Yes," they said. "We swear and we promise that we won't touch a thing until you come back."

Baby crawled away as fast as he could.
Five hours later, he could no longer be
seen through the bushes.

Mother and Father waited. And waited.

After a year they began to get hungry.

But they kept their promise to Baby.

Another year passed. And then another.

They grew hungrier and hungrier.

Finally Mother said, "One sandwich won't hurt."

"No," said Father. "We promised to wait until

Baby comes back."

15

Another year passed and then another.

They began to get ravenous. Still they waited.

At last Mother said, "It's been six years.

We have to eat *something!*"

"Well," said Father, "I guess Baby won't mind."

They each reached for a sandwich, but just
as they were about to start eating, Baby
popped his head out of the bushes.
"Aha! I knew it!" he said.
"I knew you would cheat!

It's a good thing I didn't go back for
that can opener!"

The Dog and the Cake

One day a dog walked into a bakery.

"Can you bake me a special cake?" he asked.

"What kind of cake would you like?"

replied the baker.

"I want it to look like a car," said the dog,
"and money means nothing if you do a good job."
"All right," said the baker, "but you will have
to wait. I need two weeks to get the right
cake pans."
"Fine," said the dog.

WE BAKE ANYTHING

22

The dog returned two weeks later.

The baker proudly presented the cake.

"Oh dear," said the dog. "It won't do
at all. This is a Ford and I wanted a
Chevrolet. But it is my fault and I will
pay you to fix it."

"Well," said the baker, "as long as you
pay me. Come back in two weeks and it will
be ready."

"Fine," said the dog.

The dog returned two weeks later.

The baker proudly presented the cake.

"Well," said the baker, "how do you

like your Chevrolet?"

"Oh dear," said the dog. "This car has two doors, and I wanted four. But I should have told you, so I'll pay you to fix it."

"Well," sighed the baker, "as long as you pay me. Come back in a week and the cake will be ready."

"Fine," said the dog.

The dog returned one week later.

The baker proudly presented the cake.

The dog looked at it carefully.

"Does this model come with seat belts?"
he asked.

"Yes," said the baker. "But you did not
ask for seat belts."

"Oh dear," said the dog. "I should have asked, so I will pay you to fix it."

"All right," sighed the baker, "as long as you pay me. Come back in a week and the cake will be ready."

"Good," said the dog.

The dog returned one week later.

The baker proudly presented the cake.

"It is wonderful," said the dog.

"It is just what I wanted."

"Good!" said the baker.

"Shall I have it delivered?"

"No," said the dog.

"Well then, I'll put it in a box for

you to take home."

"Don't bother," said the dog as he jumped
up on the counter. "I'll eat it right here."

King of the Beasts!
KING OF THE JUNGLE!

One day a proud young lion
went stalking through the jungle.
The day was warm, the air was clean,
and the lion felt good.

Every so often he stopped and roared,

"I am King of the Beasts!

KING OF THE JUNGLE!"

Soon he saw an elephant coming down the path.
"Look at you!" shouted the lion. "You have a
tail in front and a tail in back. And your ears
don't stay on your head. And I should know,
for I am King of the Beasts!
KING OF THE JUNGLE!"

The elephant just looked and
listened and walked on down the path.

The lion roared and roared

and continued on his way.

Soon he saw a
laughing hyena hiding
behind a tree.

"And you!" shouted the lion. "You have spots on your face. Four toes on each foot. And all you do is laugh. And I should know, for I am King of the Beasts! KING OF THE JUNGLE!"

40

The hyena looked and listened
and ran to another tree.

The lion roared and roared and continued
on his way.

Soon he saw a snake moving out
from under a stone.

"And look at you," shouted the lion,
"down on your belly, crawling in the dirt.
All you do is hiss. And you keep slipping
out of your skin. And I should know,
for I am King of the Beasts!
KING OF THE JUNGLE!"

The snake looked up and

Hissssssssssssssssed

and glided down the path.

The lion beat his chest.

His tail shot up in the air.

Then, under a leaf, he saw a tiny flicker.
He turned the leaf over. There on the
ground was a teeny tiny mouse.
The lion looked at the mouse.
The mouse looked at the lion.

"And you!" shouted the lion. "You are nothing! You can't fight! You can hardly be seen. And all you do is squeak. And I should know, for I am King of the Beasts!
KING OF THE JUNGLE!"

The little mouse gave the lion a dirty look.

"I'm not always this small," he squeaked.

"I've been sick."